Reading Together

SCARY PARTY

Read it together

Scary Party is a colourful, humorous invitation to a monster party. By reading the book together you can join in the fun and discover that it's not so scary after all.

What's another part of your body?

Using the pictures, children can try to guess what's coming up on the next page. This helps them become more confident readers.

Legs!

Let's see if they're next.

Eyes, eyes, look...

...at the eyes, dancing in the dark. OH, NO!

There is a strong rhythm running through the book which helps children remember how the story goes. With encouragement, they will begin to join in and enjoy the experience of being a reader.

When children know the story well, they can begin to match the words they say to those they can see.

The book's bold illustrations will encourage lots of talk. Talking about the pictures helps children make sense of the book and ask any questions they might have.

For my sister, Christina

First published 1998 by Walker Books Ltd
87 Vauxhall Walk, London SE11 5HJ

This edition published 2001

2 4 6 8 10 9 7 5 3 1

© 1998 Sue Hendra
Introductory and concluding notes © 2001 CLPE/LB Southwark

This book has been typeset in Alpha bold

Printed in Hong Kong

British Library Cataloguing in Publication Data:
a catalogue record for this book is available
from the British Library

ISBN 0-7445-6871-4

SCARY PARTY

Sue Hendra

WALKER BOOKS
AND SUBSIDIARIES
LONDON • BOSTON • SYDNEY

Bones, bones, look at the bones.

dancing in the dark. OH, NO!

Eyes, eyes, look at the eyes,

dancing in the dark, OH, NO!

Arms, arms, look at the arms,

dancing in the dark. OH, NO!

Legs, legs, look at the legs,

dancing in the dark. OH, NO!

Bodies, bodies, look at the bodies,

dancing in the dark. OH, NO!

Heads, heads, look at the heads,

dancing in the dark. OH, NO!

OH, NO!
OH, NO!
IT'S TOO SCARY!
TURN ON THE LIGHT!

Read it again

Monster labels
Look carefully at the pictures together, talking about what makes a monster a monster. Children can draw their own monster and, with your help, describe, count and label parts of its body.

Monster mask
You could help your child make a simple monster mask out of black paper, card or a paper plate, and they could decorate it.

Monster dance
Children can act out the story by dancing along with the monsters at the party. As you read the book aloud, they can join in by doing all the monster actions.

Monster munch
What would monsters eat at their party? Children can make modelling clay party food for hungry monsters.

Scary things
There are many scary sights and feelings in real life as well as in books and on TV. Talk together about what your child finds scary. You can begin by sharing some of your childhood fears.

Many monsters
There are monster books of all kinds: songs; poems and rhymes; stories; information books and home-made books. Real and imagined monsters are often featured on TV and videos too. Young children usually enjoy them if there's some humour and they have the reassurance of an adult. They may even have favourites.

Reading Together

Reading Together Parents' Handbook
Myra Barrs Sue Ellis

Red Books 2-4 years

Yellow Books 3-5 years

Blue Books 4-6 years

Green Books 5-7 years